NO HICKORY
NO DICKORY
NO DOCK

Also by John Agard in Viking

Laughter is an Egg

NO HICKORY
NO DICKORY
NO DOCK

A Collection of Caribbean Nursery Rhymes by
John Agard and Grace Nichols

Illustrated by Penny Dann

VIKING

*To Our Baby Daughter, Kalera,
and to all you little rhyme-lovers out there*

VIKING
Published by the Penguin Group
Penguin Books Ltd, 27 Wrights Lane, London w8 5 tz, England
Viking Penguin Inc., 40 West 23rd Street, New York, New York 10010, USA
Penguin Books Australia Ltd, Ringwood, Victoria, Australia
Penguin Books Canada Ltd, 2801 John Street, Markham, Ontario, Canada l3 r 1 b4
Penguin Books (NZ) Ltd, 182–190 Wairau Road, Auckland 10, New Zealand

Penguin Books Ltd, Registered Offices: Harmondsworth, Middlesex, England

First published 1991
1 3 5 7 9 10 8 6 4 2

Text copyright © John Agard and Grace Nichols, 1991
Illustrations copyright © Penny Dann, 1991

The moral right of the authors has been asserted

Made and printed in Great Britain by
Butler and Tanner Ltd, Frome and London

Filmset in Linotron Baskerville by
Rowland Phototypesetting Ltd, Bury St Edmunds, Suffolk

A CIP catalogue record for this book is available from the British Library

ISBN 0–670–82661–8

CONTENTS

NO HICKORY NO DICKORY
NO DOCK

Wasn't me
Wasn't me
said the little mouse
I didn't run up no clock

You could hickory me
You could dickory me
or lock me in a dock

I still say
I didn't run up no clock

Was me who ran under your bed
Was me who bit into your bread
Was me who nibbled your cheese

But please please,
I didn't run up no clock
no hickory
no dickory
no dock.

John Agard

HIPPITY-HIPPITY-HATCH

Hippity-Hippity-Hatch
my black fowl's on her patch
keeping her eggs
all cosy and warm
Hippity-Hippity-Hatch

Hippity-Hippity-Hatch
my black fowl's left her patch
her chicks have all cracked
into the world
Hippity-Hippity-Hatch

Grace Nichols

CLAP HAND FOR MAMMY

Clap hand for mammy
Till daddy come
Daddy bring cake and sugarplum
Give baby some

Baby eat all
Ain't give mammy none
Mammy get vex
Throw baby down

Traditional

JAWBONE ON THE WALL

I hung my jawbone on the wall
I did not know dem bones would fall.
Jawbone walk, Jawbone talk
Jawbone eat with a knife and fork.

Traditional

COW CHAT

Mama Moo
Papa Moo
Baby Moo
lying in the grass

Said Mama Moo
to Papa Moo
'When the grass is new
I love to chew'

'And I do too'
said Baby Moo

John Agard

SO-SO JOE

So-So Joe
de so-so man
wore a so-so suit
with a so-so shoe.
So-So Joe
de so-so man
lived in a so-so house
with a so-so view.
And when you asked
So-so Joe
de so-so man
How do you do?
So-So Joe
de so-so man
would say to you:

> Just so-so
> Nothing new.

John Agard

HERE COMES THE BRIDE

Here comes the bride
All dressed in white
White shoes and stockings
And dirty feet inside

Traditional

QUEEN FOOT-SHE-PUT

She looked so tall
In the Foot-She-Put

She looked so grand
In the Foot-She-Put

A great-great Queen
Was Foot-She-Put

The men fell down
At the Foot-She-Put

She gave such a cry
In the Foot-She-Put

They stood and shook
O the Foot-She-Put

Foot-She-Put
Foot-She-Put

There never was a queen
Like Foot-She-Put.

Grace Nichols

I WOULDN'T GO TO MISSIE
(A Slap-hand Rhyme)

I wouldn't go to Missie
Any more, more, more
There's a big fat police
At the door, door, door

He will hold me by the collar
And make me pay a dollar
And a dollar is a dollar
So I wouldn't go to Missie
Any more, more, more

Traditional

TWINKLE TWINKLE FIREFLY

Twinkle
Twinkle
Firefly
In the dark
It's you I spy

Over the river
Over the bush

Twinkle
Twinkle
Firefly
For the traveller
passing by

Over the river
Over the bush

Twinkle
Twinkle
Firefly
Lend the dark
your sparkling eye

John Agard

MOSQUITO ONE
MOSQUITO TWO

Mosquito one
mosquito two
mosquito jump
in de old man shoe

Traditional

DON'T CRY CATERPILLAR

Don't cry, Caterpillar
Caterpillar, don't cry
You'll be a butterfly – by and by.

Caterpillar, please
Don't worry 'bout a thing

'But,' said Caterpillar,
'Will I still know myself – in wings?'

Grace Nichols

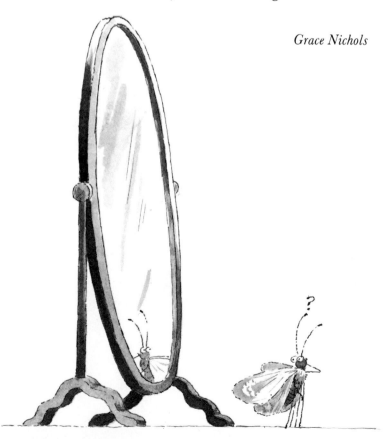

WHAT TURKEY DOING?

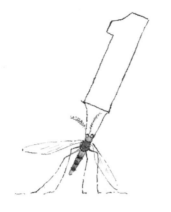

Mosquito one
mosquito two
mosquito jump
in de old man shoe

Cockroach three
cockroach four
cockroach dance thru
a crack in de floor

Spider five
spider six
spider weaving
a web of tricks

Monkey seven
monkey eight
monkey playing with
pencil and slate

Turkey nine
turkey ten
what turkey doing
in chicken pen?

John Agard

MY PARAKEET

Anyone see my parakeet, Skeet?
He's small and neat,
He's really sweet,
With his pick-pick beak,
And his turn-back feet.

Skeet, Skeet, I wouldn't tell a lie
You are the green-pearl of my eye.

Grace Nichols

INCHY PINCHY PINCHY MALADY

Inchy Pinchy Pinchy Malady
Inchy Pinchy Pinchy Malady
All the birdies fly away!

Traditional

DE POP-CORN WOULDN'T POP

De pop-corn wouldn't pop
De peas wouldn't grow
De jelly wouldn't jell
De fowlcock wouldn't crow

De bread wouldn't brown
De milk wouldn't flow
De banana wouldn't ripe
De grass wouldn't mow

Just can't tek it no more
Just can't tek it no more

Grace Nichols

SUGARCAKE BUBBLE

Sugarcake, Sugarcake
    Bubbling in a pot
Bubble, Bubble Sugarcake
    Bubble thick and hot

Sugarcake, Sugarcake
    Spice and coconut
Sweet and sticky
    Brown and gooey

I could eat the lot.

Grace Nichols

27

LONDON BRIDGE

London bridge is broken down
broken down broken down
London bridge is broken down
my fair lady

See de robbers passing by
passing by passing by
See de robbers passing by
my fair lady

What dis poor robber do
robber do robber do
What dis poor robber do
my fair lady?

He broke my lock and stole my gold
stole my gold stole my gold
He broke my lock and stole my gold
my fair lady

How many pounds will set him free
set him free set him free?
How many pounds will set him free
my fair lady?

Ten thousand pounds will set him free
set him free set him free
Ten thousand pounds will set him free
my fair lady.

Ten thousand pounds is far too much
far too much far too much
Ten thousand pounds is far too much
my fair lady.

Then off to prison we must go
we must go we must go
Then off to prison we must go
my fair lady

Traditional

DOCTOR KILL

Please remember when you're ill
not to send for Doctor Kill

If you have the mumps he'll give you more
    bumps
If you have a sore he'll give you some more

Never take a pill from this Doctor Kill
and better don't touch the medicine he pour
for his full name is
    Doctor-Kill-And-Can't-Cure
None other than
    Doctor-Kill-And-Can't-Cure.

Doctor-Kill-And-Can't-Cure
Please stay away from my door

John Agard

DUTCH GIRL
(A Slap-hand Rhyme)

I am a pretty little Dutch girl
As pretty as pretty can be
And all the boys around my square
Go crazy crazy over me

My boyfriend's name is Tommy
He come from far Ammambo
With a big red nose
And ten tippy toes
And that's the way my story goes

One day he gave me pictures
One day he gave me pears
One day he gave me fifty cents
And kicked me down the stairs

I gave him back his pictures
I gave him back his pears
I gave him back his fifty cents
And kicked him down the stairs

Traditional

31

SIR GARFIELD

Sir Garfield was his name
and cricket was his game

A bat he loved to wield
A ball he loved to swing.
See Sir Garfield
on a cricket field,
and man, you see a king

He hit one six and he hit two six
He hit three six and he hit four six
He hit five six and he hit six six

Six six in a row.
Licks-o licks-o!
Sir Garfield on de go.

John Agard

MARY-ANNE MARLEY

Mary-Anne Marley she wouldn't marry
Mary-Anne Marley she made
   her poopa angry
Mary-Anne Marley she shook her head
Mary-Anne Marley she sang instead;

Before me marry
me go hug-up mango tree
hug-up mango tree

Before me marry
me go hug-up mango tree
me go live like free-bee

A rich-rich Mister he came for to marry her
A rich-rich Mister he came for to marry her
Mary-Anne Marley she shook her head
Mary-Anne Marley she sang instead;

Before me marry
me go hug-up mango tree
hug-up mango tree

Before me marry
me go hug-up mango tree
me go live like free-bee.

Grace Nichols

ARITHMETIC

Arithmetic
Me father sick
Me teacher hit me
With a mortar stick

Traditional

ONE TWO ANANCY

ONE TWO
Anancy to you.
THREE FOUR
Never trust de score.
FIVE SIX
Always up to tricks.
SEVEN EIGHT
Can't play de game straight.
NINE TEN
Anancy, your tricky friend.

John Agard

GIVE ME FIVE

Give me five fingers of joy
Give me five fingers of joy
Give me five fingers of joy
from every jumping girl and boy

Give me five fingers of love
Give me five fingers of love
Give me five fingers of love
from the side below and above

Give me five fingers of play
Give me five fingers of play
Give me five fingers of play
I tell you that will make my day

Fingers tell a story
Fingers tell their very own story
O yes believe me
O yes believe me
Fingers tell a story
Fingers tell their very own story

Catch the morning with open hands
Catch the morning with open hands
Catch the morning with open hands
Today we leave our fists behind

John Agard

HUMPTY

Humpty Dumpty did sit on a wall
Humpty Dumpty did have a great fall
All the King's horses and all the King's men
Did try to put him together again.

But after they left
And poor Humpty had wept
Along came little Hugh
Who knew of super-glue

It took him a while
But Humpty Dumpty was back in style
(Now, Humpty's planning to run, 'The Mile')
All because of little Hugh
Who fixed him up with super-glue.

Grace Nichols

IS WHA, IS WHA, IS WHA YOU WATCHING ME FAH?

Is wha, is wha, is wha you watching me fah?
Is wha, is wha, is wha you watching me fah?
Sandfly marry to mosquito daughter
Make de cake with some dirty water.
Is wha, is wha, is wha you watching me fah?

Traditional

MAMA-WATA

Down by the seaside
when the moon is in bloom
sits Mama-Wata
gazing up at the moon

She sits as she combs
her hair like a loom
she sits as she croons
a sweet kind of tune

But don't go near Mama-Wata
when the moon is in bloom
for sure she will take you
down to your doom.

Grace Nichols

BROWN-RIVER BROWN-RIVER

Brown-River
Brown-River
Why do you run
You must be trying
To catch-up with someone?

O I'm on my way
To catch-up with the sea
But however fast I run
There's always more of me
Always more of me.

Grace Nichols

WOODPECKER

Carving
tap/tap
music
out of
tap/tap
tree trunk
keep me
busy
whole day
tap/tap
long

tap/tap
pecker
birdsong
tap/tap
pecker
birdsong

tree bark
is tap/tap
drumskin
fo me beak
I keep
tap/tap
rhythm
fo forest
heartbeat

tap/tap
chisel beak
long
tap/tap
honey leak
song
pecker/tap
tapper/peck
pecker
birdsong

John Agard

45

WASHING-UP DAY

Clothes in a tub
rub rub rub.
Clothes in a tub
rub rub rub.
Hand in soapy water-o
Hand in soapy water-o

Clothes in a tub
rub-um squeeze-um.
Clothes in a tub
rub-um wring-um.
Hand in soapy water-o
Hand in soapy water-o

Clothes in a tub
come nice and clean,
but I saving up
me money
for washing-machine

John Agard

TUMBLE DRYING

Spin Spin Spin
tumble tumble tumble
short and tall
big and small
all go round and round

Spin Spin Spin
tumble tumble tumble
nylon and cotton
zip-up and button
all go round and round

Grace Nichols

MISS ROSIE AND MISS BOSIE

Miss Rosie and Miss Bosie
hanging out clothes,
Miss Rosie gave Miss Bosie
a stamp on her toes.

Next thing you know
they exchanging blows.
Miss Bosie twisting
Miss Rosie nose.

A policeman passing by
Said, 'Come with me to the station'
But they grabbed him by the collar
And called him 'Botheration'.

Grace Nichols

ABNA BABNA
(A Counting-out Rhyme)

Abna Babna
Lady-Snee
Ocean potion
Sugar and tea
Potato roast
And English toast
out goes she.

Traditional

ONE FINE DAY IN THE MIDDLE OF THE NIGHT

One fine day in the middle of the night
Two dead men began to fight
Two blind men to see fair play
One dumb man to shout hurray
A lame-foot donkey passing by
Kicked the man in he left right eye.

Traditional

PUSSY IN DE MOONLIGHT

Pussy in de moonlight
Pussy in de zoo
Pussy never come home
Till half past two

Traditional

WHO IS DE GIRL?

Who is de girl dat kick de ball
then jump for it over de wall?

Sally-Ann is a girl so full-o zest
Sally-Ann is a girl dat just can't rest

Who is de girl dat pull de hair
of de bully and make him scare?

Sally-Ann is a girl so full-o zest
Sally-Ann is a girl dat just can't rest

Who is de girl dat bruise she knee
when she fall from de mango tree?

Sally-Ann is a girl so full-o zest
Sally-Ann is a girl dat just can't rest

Who is de girl dat set de pace
When boys and girls dem start to race?

Sally-Ann is a girl so full-o zest
Sally-Ann is a girl dat just can't rest

John Agard

OLD MISTER GOSWELL

Old Mister Goswell
going to de well,
didn't like pinedrink
Coke or sorrel

What he liked
and I will tell
was a nice cool drink
of water from de well

Old Mister Goswell
going to de well,
couldn't be bothered
by de ice-cream bell.

Grace Nichols

THIS OLD LADY FROM CARIBEE

A certain old lady from Caribee
loved the sound of kis-ka-dee-kis-kis-ka-dee

Somewhere up in mango tree
kis-ka-dee bird
singing kis-ka-dee-kis-kis-ka-dee

Every day before her morning coffee
this old lady from Caribee
would listen for kis-ka-dee-kis-kis-ka-dee

Kis-ka-dee sound would start her day
and she wondered
if this was how these kis-ka-dees pray

And as the years went by
and she could no longer see –
this old lady from Caribee

still heard the sound of kis-ka-dee
kis-kis-ka-dee
kis-kis-ka-dee

John Agard

A-SO SHE SAY

Tom Tom the piper's son
stole a pig
A-SO DEM SAY
and away he run
A-SO DEM SAY
the pig was eat
A-SO DEM SAY
and Tom was beat
A-SO DEM SAY
but my teacher say
A-SO SHE SAY
it ought to be
the pig was eaten
and Tom was beaten
A-SO SHE SAY
and my teacher does talk sweet
and my teacher does write neat
and my teacher don't eat pig meat
A-SO SHE SAY

John Agard

NO MORE LATIN
(Chanted by Children when School is Closing)

No more Latin
No more French
No more sitting
On de old school bench

No more licks
To make me cry
No more eyewater
To come out me eye

Traditional

57

SKIPPING ROPE SPELL

Turn rope turn
Don't trip my feet
Turn rope turn
for my skipping feet

Turn rope turn
turn round and round
Turn in the air
Turn on the ground

One for your high
One for your low.
Turn rope turn
Not too fast, not too slow

Turn rope turn
turn to the north
turn to the south.
But please rope, please,
Don't make me out

John Agard

JOHNNY-TOO-LAZY

Johnny-Too-Lazy wouldn't bathe he skin
Johnny-Too-Lazy wouldn't shave he chin
Johnny-Too-Lazy wouldn't brush he teeth
Johnny-Too-Lazy wouldn't wipe he feet
Johnny-Too-Lazy wouldn't comb he hair
Johnny-Too-Lazy wouldn't take a care

When Johnny-Too-Lazy was finally wed
His wife had to beat him out of bed.

Grace Nichols

IN THE LAND OF TAKE-YOUR-TIME

In the land
of Take-Your-Time
it is a crime
to hurry

In the land
of Take-Your-Time
it is a crime
to worry

In the land
of Take-Your-Time
it is a crime
to rush your meals

In the land
of Take-Your-Time
everyone walks about
on their heels

John Agard

NEIGHBOUR NEIGHBOUR

Neighbour Neighbour
lend me yuh basket

*What you going to do
with basket?*

Basket to go
to market

*What you going to do
at market?*

Market to buy
some pumpkin

*What you going to do
with pumpkin?*

Pumpkin to make
some dumplin

*What you going to do
with dumplin?*

Dumplin to give
to me darlin

Dumplin to give
to me darlin

Grace Nichols

TEN BISCUITS

Ten biscuits
In a pack
Who don't want dem
Turn their back

Back-to-Back
Sago-pap
Ten biscuits
In a pack

Traditional

DE BOTTLEMAN

Bottles! Bottles!
Bottles I buy.
Hear de bottleman cry

Long bottles
Short bottles
Fat bottles
Thin bottles

Bottles! Bottles!
Bottles I buy.
Hear de bottleman cry

Search low search high.
I buy dem wet
I buy dem dry

Run with a bottle
to de bottleman cart
when yuh hear de bottleman cry

Bottles! Bottles!
Bottles I buy

John Agard

A VERSE FROM ONE OF GUYANA'S NATIONAL SONGS

Onward upward may we ever go
Day by day in strength and beauty grow
Till at length each of us may show
What Guyana's sons and daughters can be.

CHILDREN'S VERSION OF THE SAME VERSE

Onward upward Mary had a goat
Day by day she tied it with a rope
Till at length de goat buss de rope
And Mary had to run behind it

Traditional

65

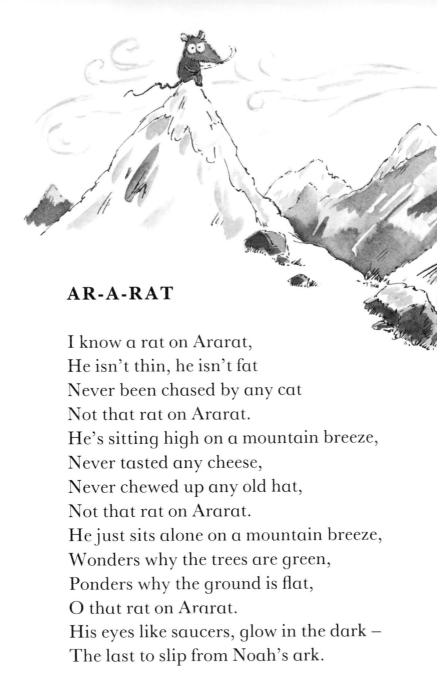

AR-A-RAT

I know a rat on Ararat,
He isn't thin, he isn't fat
Never been chased by any cat
Not that rat on Ararat.
He's sitting high on a mountain breeze,
Never tasted any cheese,
Never chewed up any old hat,
Not that rat on Ararat.
He just sits alone on a mountain breeze,
Wonders why the trees are green,
Ponders why the ground is flat,
O that rat on Ararat.
His eyes like saucers, glow in the dark –
The last to slip from Noah's ark.

Grace Nichols

LADYBIRD LADYBIRD

Ladybird
Ladybird

Have you heard
the birds
laughing?
They say you can't sing

But ladybird
I don't care
if you can't sing,
I like how you move
your red and black wing.

John Agard

67

TURTLE MYRTLE

Turtle Myrtle
was slow but could hurtle
as only a hurtling turtle can

She hurtle in water
She hurtle on sand
She hurtle in grass
She hurtle on land
as only a hurtling turtle can

'Myrtle, Myrtle,' said Mother Turtle
'hurtle not fuh turtle, take-care, Myrtle
yuh ain't afraid yuh brittle back buckle?'

But Turtle Myrtle would only chuckle
and show Mother Turtle another hurtle.
                              O Myrtle.

Grace Nichols

GRANNY

It so nice to have a Granny
when you've had it from yuh Mammy
and you feeling down and dammy

It so nice to have a Granny
when she brings you bread and jammy
and says, 'Tell it all to Granny.'

Grace Nichols

MOSQUITO MOSQUITO

Mosquito mosquito, why do you go
  everywhere I go?
Well my child, it's blood I follow
Mosquito mosquito, biting people, is that all
  you know?
Yes my child, biting people is all I know.

Well mosquito, don't bite me, bite Uncle Joe
He always boasting he sweet from head to
  toe.

John Agard

SCHOOL CALL IN

Ting-a-Ling-a-Ling
School call in
Belly haul in

Ting-a-Ling-a-Ling
School over
Belly turn over

Traditional

PUMPKIN PUMPKIN

Pumpkin
Pumpkin
Where have you been?

I been to Hallowe'en
to frighten the queen

Pumpkin
Pumpkin
how did you do it?

With two holes for my eyes
and a light
in me head

I frightened the queen
right under her bed!

John Agard

BABY-K RAP RHYME

My name is Baby-K
An dis is my rhyme
Sit back folks
While I rap my mind;

Ah rocking with my homegirl,
My Mommy
Ah rocking with my homeboy,
My Daddy
My big sister, Les, an
My Granny,
Hey dere people – my posse
I'm the business
The ruler of the nursery

poop po-doop
poop-poop po-doop
poop po-doop
poop-poop po-doop

Well, ah soaking up de rhythm
Ah drinking up my tea
Ah bouncing an ah rocking
On my Mommy knee
So happy man so happy

poop po-doop
poop-poop po-doop
poop po-doop
poop-poop po-doop

Wish my rhyme wasn't hard
Wish my rhyme wasn't rough
But sometimes, people
You got to be tough

Cause dey pumping up de chickens
Dey stumping down de trees
Dey messing up de ozones
Dey messing up de seas
Baby-K say, stop dis –
please, please, please

poop po-doop
poop-poop po-doop
poop po-doop
poop-poop po-doop

Now am splashing in de bath
With my rubber duck
Who don't like dis rhyme
Kiss my baby-foot
Babies everywhere
Join a Babyhood

Cause dey hotting up de globe, man
Dey hitting down de seals
Dey killing off de ellies
For dere ivories
Baby-K say, stop dis –
please, please, please

poop po-doop
poop-poop po-doop
poop po-doop
poop-poop po-doop

Dis is my Baby-K rap
But it's a kinda plea
What kinda world
Dey going to leave fuh me?
What kinda world
Dey going to leave fuh me?

Poop po-doop.

Grace Nichols

75

INDEX OF FIRST LINES

79